CHRISTIAN SHORT STORIES

RL
Literary productions

Biblical quotations

Preface

What is the Christian life?

How does it really take place day by day?

How to know if what we are doing is according to Jesus' commandments?

How to know if we are being good Christians?

These are very hard questions to be answered. Sometimes, we think we are doing the best, but will it be the best for Jesus?

Jesus does not come to face us directly because we could not reply to Him. However, He left His word for us to consult.

If we are disposed to understand and obey, it will lead us to the right path.

Table of Contents

The Judgment Seat of Christ

For we must all appear before the judgment seat of Christ, that each one may receive what is due him for the things done while in the body, whether good or bad. (2 Corinthians 5:10)

Then took place the day of the Last Judgment, the day when everyone should appear before Jesus, for Him to examine the things done by each one of us.

There were two men at the entrance of the court, Paul and Dennis. The first one has the name of a missionary and preacher, coming from a Christian family, he was always involved with the church. However, his involvement was not wholehearted. He did everything like an obligation to his parents. Throughout the years, he was gradually moving away from the church's activities. He went to the services every fifteen days, or once a month. The distancing was not because of work or study; it was because of laziness and discouragement. Anything was a reason for him not to go to the church, even the rain or heat. Unlike the apostle, this Paul did not preach for anybody, nor fasted; he prayed a little or virtually nothing and did not help anyone in anything. He always thought the fact of being a Sunday Christian[1] was enough for his life.

---

[1] Among Christians, this expression indicates a person who only goes to church and participates on Sundays (the day of the main service) and does not do anything else related to the Christian life.

Dennis had the name of a god from Greek mythology. His life was always very complicated. His father was an alcoholic, and his mother was a compulsive smoker. When he was a teenager, Dennis was introduced to the Gospel and always prayed and sought incessantly for the conversion of his family. After some time, his father, mother, and brothers converted to the Gospel. Dennis was always very hardworking to preach the Gospel; he was a living witness of the transforming power of the word of God. He assisted in the church as a deacon, street evangelist, and in any activity the church needed. He was always willing to help everyone that required it. Only during the college period did he partially move away from some church activities.

Now, they both are before the judgment seat of Christ, and each one will be judged according to their acts.

They are seated waiting for Christ's arrival to judge them.

Dennis had the same appearance when he was a young adult, tan skin, thin, average height, short black hair, and light brown eyes.

Paul also had the same appearance when he was a young adult, thin, average height, dark brown skin, almost shaved black hair, and brown eyes.

Jesus gets into the room, and immediately Dennis kneels, recognizing his condition as a sinner, and the authority of Jesus.

Paul thought, *This man must be a great sinner, that's why he's like that. Fortunately, I'm not like that. I always walked righteously before the Lord.*

Noticing the arrogance of Paul, Jesus said in an energetic tone, "Woe to you, scribes and Pharisees!"

One more time, Paul thought, *For sure, this is for that man.*

Jesus shook his head negatively and passed the hand over his face.

He entered the court and called Paul, this one thought, *The best ones are always the first chosen.*

Paulo entered the room and did not show any reverence to the person of Jesus. Paul acted as if he had known Jesus for a long time, and they were very intimate.

Jesus looked strangely at Paul's attitude and said, "I don't understand. Why are you behaving like that?"

Paul smiled and said with excitement, "Master! I have known you since I was a child. We're best friends."

Jesus was amazed, "Best friends? Are you sure of it?"

Paul replied with confidence, "Of course, Lord! Since I was too young, I heard about your name and was baptized in adolescence and…"

"Oh! Then you are talking about that. Now, I got it."

Paul thought, *He must have forgotten. There are too many people…*

Immediately, Jesus said in a loud voice, "I know by name all the sheep that my Father gave me, and all of them know my voice."

Paul thought, ironically, *I already know all of it.*

Jesus seated in the judge's chair and said with authority, "Sit in the dock."

Paul was amazed at Jesus's request and said, "Me? In the dock?"

Jesus replied firmly in a reproachful tone, "Yes! Now!"

Paul walked to the chair and said with discouragement, "Alright. You don't need to scream."

Jesus took an enormous book and began to peruse it like he was searching for something.

Paul did not understand what Jesus was doing.

After perusing a little, Jesus said, "There is nothing about you in the Book of Life[2]."

Paul was confused; Jesus continued, "Let's see what you did in your life."

Paul replied with confidence, "But the Lord already knows everything!"

"Of course, I know. It seems you don't know what you did in your life."

Paul said confidently, "For sure, I know what I did in my life!"

For testing Paul, Jesus said, "If you know everything you did. Then, tell me."

Paul began to tell the history of his life, "Lord, I virtually grew up inside the church. I was always very participative. I was from the musical group; I was always involved with the church. I was a very

---

[2] In Christianity, the Book of Life is the book in which God records the names of every person who is destined for Heaven and the World to Come (better and perfect).

The Book of Life is quoted seven times in the Book of Revelation (3:5, 13:8, 17:8, 20:12, 20:15, 21:27, 22:19)

good man, I never killed nor stole, nor prostituted me. I worked honestly. I always gave my tithe[3], the offerings. I participated in the Lord's Supper[4]. Likewise, I was practically a Christian example."

Jesus interrupted him and said reproachfully, "An example not to be followed!"

Paul was amazed by the reply, "But how so?"

Jesus replied calmly, "Paul, I understand all your thoughts, and at this moment, I see that you firmly believe you were a good person and deserve to be saved. However, let's detail what you said. We'll see if your life was exemplary."

"All right. Let's see it."

"You said you grew up inside the church, but let's see some images of your childhood."

On a screen, in front of them, a video was exhibited of Paul's childhood.

He was lying in his bedroom. Paul's mother, a tall and thin woman with brown skin, mid-back length hair, and brown eyes, knocks on the door and calls him, "Lil Paul, go and take a shower, so we can go to church."

---

[3] Financial contribution to help churches. The value corresponds to ten percent of what is received by the person.

[4] One Christian rite that is considered an ordinance. According to the New Testament, the rite was instituted by Jesus Christ during the Last Supper; giving his disciples bread and wine during a Passover meal, he commanded them to do this in his memory; referring to the bread as his body and the cup of wine as the new covenant in his blood. (Matthew 26:26-29, Mark 14:22:25, Luke 22:14-20, 1 Corinthians 11:23-26)

He replied, making a tantrum, "I don't wanna. I don't go. It's too boring!"

The mother entered the bedroom and said reproachfully, "Hey boy, don't say it! We must go to thank God for everything he makes for us."

"But I can thank Him here."

"But in the church, we especially thank Him, without distractions."

"Oh no, mom! I won't go." Paul continued making tantrums.

She said in a serious tone, "If you don't go, you'll run out of video games."

Fearing mother's threat, he agreed, "Alright. I'm going."

During the service, Paul was frowning in the church, very sullen.

Jesus turns to Paul and says, "Was it like that you grew up in the church?"

Paul tried to argue, "But it was only…"

"It wasn't only that day. Virtually, every day was the same thing."

Paul would go to say something, but Jesus said, "Don't even try to say this was just when you were a child. During your adolescence, you didn't go to church out of love for me. You had other interests. And it was because of these interests you were very participative," Jesus said ironically. "Let's see your participation in the church."

They watch another video. Paul was a teenager and participated in the musical group. However, his participation was only by the interest to be recognized by other people, especially girls. While he was playing or singing, he was staring at the girls on the benches, and he always tried to get close to them. He always had the same conversation.

He got close to a girl about his age and said, "You sing so well! I think you could participate in the musical group."

She was flattered by Paul's words. And he continued, "Let's set a day for us to train more."

Indeed, his real intention was to have a date with the girl. Paul always did it, sometimes worked and sometimes did not. But he did not change.

Jesus looked at him with a reproachful expression and said, "What do you tell me in your defense?"

Paul was extremely constrained and tried to justify himself, "That is… It's. Lord, I was a teen…"

Jesus interrupted him, "I know you were a teenager, immature, and had many wills. But why didn't you ever ask me for help? If you had asked for help, I would have helped you to overcome these wills. I would send my Holy Spirit to guide you through the right path. You preferred to be dominated by your desires!"

Paul lowered his head and reflected a bit.

Jesus continued, "The next thing you said, 'I never killed nor stole, nor prostituted me. I worked honestly.'"

Paul said firmly, "This one, I'm sure I made everything right."

Jesus contested, "Are you sure?"

Paul replies with doubt, "Yes. I think so."

Jesus replied, "You said you never killed; let's see it."

It starts a video where Paul is walking on the sidewalk and sees a beggar seated on the ground, very dirty and begging.

Immediately, Paul thinks, *I'm gonna pass looking to the other side, then, he doesn't look into my face and ask me anything.*

And Paul did like that, and after passing, he heard the beggar saying, "God is seeing all things."

Paul stopped for a moment but quickly followed his path without giving any importance to that man.

Jesus said in a reproachful tone, "Is this what I taught in the gospels? Is this the commandment I ordered?"

Paul lowered the head. And Jesus continued questioning in the same tone, "What did I teach? What is my commandment? I know that you know, then, say it!"

Paul replied with discouragement, "Love your neighbor as yourself[5]."

Jesus replied, exalted, "Where was the love to the neighbor at that moment? You say you are good because you haven't killed anybody. But know when you turn your back to those who are asking for help, it isn't much different than to draw a gun and shoot at a person. Basically, the two are hurting and mistreating lives."

---

[5] Matthew 22:39, Mark 12:31

Paul was without a reply and impacted by Jesus' words. He continued in a calm tone, "You said that you never stole, haven't you?"

"Yes."

And Jesus contested, "Let's confirm this."

One more video is exhibited. This time, Paul was making a clandestine connection in electricity cables. And it was also shown that he purchased an electronic device to get paid TV signals without payment.

Jesus said, "Was this honest? Or correct?"

Paul replied sadly, "It wasn't, Lord."

"I taught, 'Give to Caesar what is Caesar's, and to God what is God's[6].'"

Paul one more time noticed he was being good in his own eyes and not before the eyes of the Lord.

Jesus continued, "And about paid TV, I won't even comment about what you watched. You know what it is. Now let's see a very interesting part. You said that you've never prostituted."

Paul said, concerned, "It comes to a trag…"

Jesus interrupted him, "There is a tragedy coming! Let's see."

Another video was exhibited. This time, Paul was singing and playing secular songs with explicit content. He wanted to succeed and get too much money with music.

---

[6] Matthew 22:21, Mark 12:17, Luke 20:25

And Jesus said, "You may not have practiced sexual prostitution. But you prostituted the gifts I gave you. You left the church's musical group and wanted a secular and worldly life."

Paul tried to justify, "But, Lord! I needed…"

Jesus interrupted in a loud voice, "I needed to pay my bills. Everybody always says this. Mainly those who do dishonorable jobs. People don't trust when they read, 'But seek first his kingdom and his righteousness, and all these things will be given to you as well[7]'. I didn't command anybody to be idle, but the Kingdom of God must be the priority in people's lives. And may they not do shameful things to get money."

Paul was completely terrified by what he heard from Jesus. He already could not argue. And Jesus continued, "Let's see your honest work."

Another video about Paul's life is exhibited. This time, he was at work at an office. A middle-aged white man arrived and said, "Paul, I need you to make a report, but I need urgency."

He replied, "I wanna help you, but see my situation. There is a queue and other demands. Then, it's hard to prioritize your report."

The man said, "I'll buy you a bar of chocolate."

Paul excitedly replied, "Now, your demand is the first one in the queue."

---

[7] Matthew 6:33

And Paul made the task quickly after the bribe promise.

Jesus questioned him, "Is this honest work? Accepting bribes to do your duty."

He tried to justify, "But my job…"

And Jesus completed ironically, "But my job is very bad," And said in a firm tone, "Everyone always says this. If the job is bad, seek another, study to improve, or do something in life. But don't sin because of it."

Every moment that passed, Paul noticed that his situation was getting more complicated. And Jesus continued in a firm tone,

"You are concerned, don't you? Did you think it would be easy? Did you think that being more or less is enough for me? But it isn't!"

Then, Jesus said in a smoother tone, "Let's continue. You also said that you gave tithe and offerings rightly."

"Yes. This one there is no way to have done wrong."

"There is a way. Let's see it."

Another video is exhibited. This time, Paul was delivering the tithe and his offering in an envelope. When he would deposit it, he thought, *I'm giving so much. I could do many things with this money.*

Paul stood with the envelope, thinking if he would deposit it or not. Because of the people seeing, he deposited. While he was backing to his seat, he thought, *How much money…*

Jesus said, "You gave the tithes and offerings with a heavy heart;

you didn't do it willingly."

Paul tried to justify, "But Lord! The mon…"

Jesus interrupted him and said firmly, "The money was running out. I needed more. It's always the same story. I'm going to ask you two things. Have you ever run out of something?"

"I haven't."

"Have I made your debts? Or was it me who made them rise from nowhere?"

Paul replied in a discouraged tone, "You haven't, Lord."

Jesus said firmly, "If the money was running out, it should take on less debt or get a better job. It was simple. Then, you wouldn't sin when you deliver tithes and offerings."

Jesus said calmly, "Now, there's only one of the things you said, the participation in the Lord's Supper."

Paul had nothing else to argue with Jesus, then, he said, discouraged, "Lord, show my mistakes."

And Jesus said with happiness, "Now we are making some progress. Let's see the video."

It was exhibited a video of Paul's day-by-day. Too many small talks, gossip, fights with church members, etc.

He usually participated on the day of the Lord's Supper like nothing had happened.

Jesus said, "You know that was for your own condemnation, don't you? Although people in the church didn't know, I always knew everything."

Paul had already accepted his destiny. He said, discouraged, "Then, I suppose this is my end, but before I go, Lord, tell me one thing. Is it possible for someone to do what I said I did, but in the right way?"

Jesus says calmly, "Yes, it's possible. I knew you would ask this. To reply to you, let's call the man who is outside."

Jesus said in a loud voice, "Dennis, please, come in."

Dennis entered, knelt, and said, "Lord, forgive me because I'm a sinner."

Jesus got close to him, took his hand, and said, "Get up, my son. All your sins are forgiven."

Dennis replied, glorifying Jesus, "Glory to thy Holy Name, Lord Jesus! Forever is the king of salvation!"

Paul observed and noticed a significant difference between them.

Jesus said, "Dennis, sit here, let's see your life."

Dennis sat in a special chair, like a throne.

One video was exhibited, and Jesus narrated the story, "Dennis had a very hard childhood, with an alcoholic father and a smoker mother. He was always got used to the smell of drinks and cigarettes. However, he never wanted any of them. During adolescence, he learned about the Gospel through an evangelistic project in his neighborhood."

Paul interrupted, "Excuse me, Lord, I know this project and even participated in it."

Jesus replied, "It's true, Paul, this was how Dennis knew salvation, and through his life, his entire family knew me, and too many others knew me. Let's see the continuation of Dennis' life."

The continuation of the video showed Paul evangelizing people in the project, and Dennis was among the evangelized ones. This was a huge surprise for Paul.

The video also showed Dennis' involvement with the work of the church, and his attention to everyone. At this moment, it was shown that Dennis gave attention to the beggar that Paul despised. Then, it is exhibited Dennis praying with a woman, and after that, his marriage. All of Dennis' life was dedicated to the Lord and the commandments.

Paul realized how much he lacked in dedication to the Kingdom of God.

Jesus said, "Dennis, here is the crown of life, reserved to those who kept my commandments and its justice."

Jesus put the crown on Dennis' head. He got up and followed walking with Jesus to the light, the eternal life.

Everything got dark, and Paul began to scream desperately, "No! Lord, don't let me perish! No! I don't wanna the eternal death."

Suddenly, Paul heard someone saying, "Wake up, are you okay?"

Paul woke up scared and said, "Where am I?"

A middle-aged black woman replied, "In the church. You napped during the sermon and lost one great preaching about the Last Judgment."

Paul noticed that everything was a dream. And when he remembered what happened, knelt and began to cry and asked for God's forgiveness, "Lord, forgive me. I'll be a better person in all senses."

The people in the church observed the scene and did not understand anything.

Paul kept this dream in his heart and was a very correct Christian until the day of his death.

What is the Meaning of Christmas?

Some children were seated on the sidewalk talking about Christmas. Alice, a light brown girl with curly black hair and brown eyes, said with excitement, "This year I'll gain too many gifts! I wrote a letter to Santa Claus, and I'm sure that he will bring everything I asked for. iPhone, iPad, laptop, a new bike, many clothes, and shoes."

Larissa, a dark brown girl with past shoulder straight hair and light brown eyes, also said with excitement, "I'll also gain many things! Too many expensive gifts! I've asked for everything, cell phone, tablet, and big-screen television."

Victor, a brown boy with buzz-cut black hair and dark brown eyes, said, "How are you so sure that you'll gain so many things?"

Larissa said, "I was a good girl the entire year and behaved well; I didn't argue with my parents, and I did everything right."

Alice said, "I also did everything right; I helped my mom when she needed me; I was a good daughter the entire year."

Victor was not convinced and said, "But to do this is our duty. After all, our parents give us a house, food, love, affection, and everything we need."

Alice disagreed and said in an energetic tone, "It's not our duty! We do this for Santa Claus to bring the gifts."

Victor insisted firmly, "It is our duty!"

Larissa questioned Victor, "And you, Victor, what did you ask

Santa Claus?"

"Nothing. He doesn't exist and can't bring anything for anyone."

Larissa and Alice said reproachfully, "This is a lie!"

Alice continued in the same tone, "He exists! It's because of him that there is Christmas!"

Victor said in a serious tone, "That's not true! Christmas exists because of someone real and more special than Santa Claus."

The girls asked, "Who?"

"Jesus Christ. It's because of him that Christmas exists and everything there is in the world."

The girls were confused, and Alice asked, "Does Jesus bring gifts?"

"He brings something better, love, forgiveness, peace, and everything good for people."

Alice said, "If he brings all these things, then he is someone very good. Where does he live?"

"He lives together with God, in the sky."

Larissa asked, "In the sky? In the clouds?"

Victor said, "Larissa and Alice, I don't know how to answer everything to you. Let's go to my house, and there, my father will explain everything."

The children went to Victor's house. At the gate, he said to his father, "Dad. Alice and Larissa were talking about Christmas and Santa Claus, and I told them that Jesus is the true reason for Christmas."

Charles, a light brown man with average height, buzz-cut hair, and brown eyes, replied, "Very well, Victor. I imagine you brought them here because they were asking hard questions, weren't they?"

"That's it, dad."

"Let's get in, and I'll explain to you."

Everyone entered the house and sat in the living room. Charles said, "I'll tell you the true reason for Christmas, however, for your better understanding, I have to tell you the entire history."

Alice and Larissa replied, "Alright."

"If you have any doubts, you can interrupt me. At the beginning of everything there was nothing, no sky, no water, no world. Then, God created all things that exist, the animals, the plants, the sun, the moon, and everything else."

Larissa raised her hand and asked, "Did God do everything alone? How did he get it?"

"Larissa, God is Almighty, and he can do all things. Tell me something that you think is impossible to happen."

Larissa thought and said, "Hmm… May my parents stop the fights."

"God can make that happen as long as they ask for his help."

"That's cool! I'll tell them this."

"Tell them, and everything will be different in your house. But continuing. After creating all things, God created people. From the beginning, he has always shown much love and kindness to everyone. God helped in everything the people needed. And like that, it was for a long time. Even when people didn't do what God asked, he always had patience and taught the right path again."

Alice interrupted, "So, was it from God's creation that Christmas came about?"

"It wasn't. Christmas is related to the most important event in the history of humanity. Christmas is related to the birth of Jesus Christ."

Alice said, "Was he born on the twenty-fifth of December?"

"Don't. This date was chosen by people. The exact date of Jesus' birth is unknown. We know that he was born more than two thousand years ago. Because of it, we are in the year two thousand twenty-one after Jesus' birth."

"I got it. Who exactly was Jesus?"

"Jesus is the Son of God. He is God in the form of a person. He was on Earth and taught many things to the people. He showed them the true meaning of forgiveness. He taught that we must have love for all people, no matter who they are. Jesus showed the path to do God's will."

Larissa said, "And what happened to Jesus?"

"Many people didn't believe in what he had said and decided to hurt him. He was murdered."

Alice said with sadness, "Was he so good and has died? People were very bad at that time."

"But Jesus' death was temporary. After three days, he was resurrected and…"

"What is to resurrect?" Larissa said because she did not understand.

"It's to come back to life after someone has died. And after that, he went back to God, his father. Since then, all people who believe in Jesus wait for the day that he'll return and will lead everyone to heaven, where there will be peace forever."

Victor said, "Did you understand why Christmas exists?"

They replied, "Yes."

Larissa said, "And Santa Claus and the gifts?"

Charles said, "I'll explain to you. Santa Claus is just a legend created from the history of a man who distributed gifts in December's month. However, this man wasn't magic. He was only a kind person. And over the years, people added things to his history, the reindeer, his living place, the color, and many other things."

Larissa said, "I got it. Then, is it wrong to gain and give gifts at Christmas?"

"It's not wrong if you do it right. The gift must be given to people whom you love and consider very special. And you must give the gift yourself and not believe that Santa Claus will give. And the most important is to tell people the true meaning of Christmas, the birth of Jesus Christ."

Larissa said, "Leave it on me. Now, I'm gonna tell everybody the truth about Christmas."

Alice completed, "Me too."

Charles said, "That's great! Now, I think you must go to your houses."

They replied, "That's true."

Larissa said, "Before I go, could you explain how I talk with God to help my parents?"

"Of course! Let's pray together. Close your eyes and repeat with me."

Larissa closed her eyes and repeated after Charles, "Lord God, I ask the Lord to help my parents to get along, and may they stop fighting and be more loving to each other. Amen."

The girls returned to their houses, happy about what they had learned.

One History

The story says that a baby was born in a very poor community, which was much awaited by all who heard about his birth.

The baby was born in an inappropriate place because there was no other place available. His birth was something ordinary, trivial, without much immediate importance. Some people who were already waiting for him went to visit his mother and gave him some gifts.

As time passed, the baby grew up and became a boy, but he was a different boy; he liked to study subjects related to his community. When he was an adult, he left home and passed through many difficulties, hunger, cold, and provocations. But he never lost hope that there would be better days.

He began to speak about laws and showed how much all the people were away from what was right and truthful. Many of his speeches strongly criticized the local authorities; they had turned into corrupt ones and lived in false appearances.

He called some people to follow him, other simple and poor men, without great social importance. However, this was not a problem because he had another look upon people.

By all places that he was going, he was followed by a great crowd, who desired to receive something from him. Then, he gifted many people and talked to them about the future of his community.

The authorities, those he criticized, sought a way to arrest him before having a rebellion. They tried in many ways, but they did not get it. The unique way to arrest him was through a bribe from one of his allies.

Then, he was arrested, and unfairly accused of provoking rebellions when in fact, he was only doing what the authorities did not do for the people. In the moment of his arrest, his allies evaded, and one pretended not to know him.

In prison, he was beaten like the worst of the convicts. He was taken to a court that found no crime against him, but due to people's pressure, the court allowed his execution.

His death was very gore, being humiliated and beaten until reaching the place where he would be executed.

At the moment of his execution, he was still cursed by some people, those who mocked his words. He did not reply to the curses but gave hope to another convicted on his side.

He has died like someone who has accepted a mission. And those who followed him lost hope at the first moment.

After three days, he resurrected and showed himself to his friends, and everyone believed in his words.

Now, you know who I am talking about, Jesus Christ.

Who is God's Servant?[8]

June 2020

At a TV studio, a black middle-aged man starts the newscast, "New coronavirus pandemic impacts everyone in the society. Thousands of people lost their jobs and sources of income. This is a moment when the population needs to come together so that, together, we can get through all of this."

1

A group of people were in a meeting room to discuss actions to help needy people during the pandemic. Everyone had an enormous desire to do something to change the situation of those who needed help, but before any action, they needed to get resources.

Mark was the group's leader. He was about thirty years old, with light brown skin, straight black hair neck length, and light brown eyes. He said, "We need suggestions to get donations for needy people."

A middle-aged white woman with long gray-blond hair and blue eyes, said, "Let's ask for help in some church; they are very receptive and have the matter of love for the neighbor."

A dark brown young man, about twenty years old, with dark hair with small braids all over his head and dark brown eyes, said, "We also can ask for help from these gospel music groups; many of

---

[8] Inspired by the parable of the Good Samaritan, Luke 10:25-37.

them already do jobs like that."

The meeting continued, and everyone gave many suggestions, and each one of them was written down. In the end, Mark said with excitement, "We already have great ideas! Let's start with the church. There is one close to here; I think there is a service tomorrow, I'll confirm it today and send messages to you."

Everyone replied, "Great!"

2

The next day, Mark and the blond woman were at the church. It had a huge structure and was very luxurious. Even the chairs were padded, like movie theater seats.

They also noticed the church's members appeared to be rich people; everyone wore elegant clothes. Only they were in casual clothes.

After the service, they sought the pastor to talk. He was close to the altar talking with other people. Mark got close and said, "Good evening, excuse me, pastor, how are you?"

The pastor, a middle-aged white man, bald, with light brown eyes, replied, "Good evening, I'm fine."

The pastor noticed their appearance and said, "You aren't from our community, are you?"

"No, we aren't. We're part of an organization that seeks to help needy people."

"This is a very beautiful work. Congratulations!"

"Thank you. We're here exactly to talk about this. We're collecting donations to help the people who are in difficulty during the pandemic."

"Too many people need help in this period."

"We think the pastor could help us with something or ask for help from the church members."

The pastor changed his expression and said seriously, "I think your attitude is too interesting, but unfortunately, we can't help."

Mark was amazed about the pastor's negative, "But, why not? Your church seems so rich."

The pastor smiled and said, "We're really a church very blessed by God."

"If you're very blessed, you should bless the others as well."

"See this big structure, and to keep this, there are many expenses. And with the pandemic, the profit, I mean, the donations decreased. Then, we can't assume any commitment to help anyone."

Mark was dissatisfied with the answer and said, "I thought that helping the neighbor was the church's mission."

The people close to them got silent when they heard this critique. Mark's partner was embarrassed by his speech, and she said in a reproachful tone, "Mark!"

"Joanna, I didn't say anything wrong."

The pastor got angry and said, "I think this conversation is over."

Mark said nervously, "It really is over, you, hypocrite!"

The pastor cried out nervously, "Shut up, you, brat!"

All who were still in the church heard his scream and were surprised by the pastor's tone.

Noticing the argumentation could be worse, Joanna took Mark's arm and said, "Let's go, now!"

They began to walk; Mark stopped and said in a loud voice to the whole church, "The love of Jesus Christ is too far from this place!"

Joanna rebuked him one more time, "Mark!"

They continued walking and went away, sad because of the answer received. She said, "These pastors only care about raising money and forget about people."

"Unfortunately, that's true. They are religious and forget their love for their neighbor."

3

After some days, Mark and Joanna went to talk to an evangelical singer, Hulda, who was very well-known for helping social causes. The meeting was in the studio where the singer recorded her songs. Mark and Joanna noticed she was very well-dressed as soon as they entered the meeting room. It was like she was going to a party. She wore earrings, necklaces, and bracelets; everything seemed to be very expensive. And there was a luxury brand bag on the table. Everyone sat; they were in front of her.

Hulda, a white woman with very fair skin, close to thirty-five years old, green eyes, and light blond hair waist length said with excitement, "Be very welcome! How can I help you?"

Mark said, "We appreciate your availability to receive us. Have you ever heard about our organization?"

"I haven't. Are you new?"

"Yes, we are. We started a short time ago and already could help many people."

"I think this work is very inspiring."

"Thank you. We also think your work is very inspiring. You help too many people."

"Thank you."

Joanna said, "Then, we need help for some people who are living tough times in this pandemic moment. Many are unemployed and without a source of income."

"The pandemic situation is really something very serious. But unfortunately, I can't help you."

Joanna was surprised by the answer, "Why not? You are rich and famous."

"It's exactly because of this. It's very expensive to maintain a life like mine. I've already been impacted by the pandemic. Before that, I used to present more than twenty concerts per month. And now, because of the restrictions, I'm receiving money only from social media. I don't know what to do to maintain my luxury standard of living."

Joanna took a deep breath, stood, and said nervously, "You should be ashamed of yourself! You're concerned about living a luxurious life while too many people are starving. You hypocrite! You sing one thing and live another."

Mark was impressed with Joanna's courage. She was facing a famous person.

Hulda was indignant about Joanna's words. She stood and said nervously, "And who do you think you are to say this?"

Joanna placed her right hand on her chest as a sign of pride. And she said seriously, "I'm a person who is trying to make a difference in a world that needs help! But I noticed that no help will come out from here. Let's go, Mark."

Mark got up, and they left the room. Hulda went after them and shouted, "You can't talk to me like that! I'm an important person!"

Joanna stopped and said reproachfully, "You're important to people. But people aren't important to you."

They followed their way.

4

After the requests for help were denied, the organization's members gathered only a few resources they had and decided to buy what they could and donate to needy people.

Mark and Joanna were leaving a supermarket with some plastic shopping bags. A middle-aged man with light brown skin, buzz-cut hair, and brown eyes, notices the t-shirts of the organization, and he says, "Excuse me, are you from that organization that helps needy people?"

Mark replied, "Yes, we are. Why?"

"I think your work is very interesting."

Mark said with discouragement, "Thank you."

The man noticed Mark's discouraged tone and asked, "Are you needing some kind of help?"

Joanna replied, "Yes, all help is welcome."

"What do you need?"

"Virtually everything. We have five families needing food urgently. But we didn't get almost anything until now."

"Oh, my God! What sadness! We're gonna solve it now!"

"How?"

"I'm gonna buy the things they need and donate them to you."

Mark got excited and said, "Really?"

"Of course, give me the address to deliver everything."

Mark gave a visit card to the man.

"This is the address of our organization."

The man delivered a visit card from a drink distributor company and said, "Here is my card. And anything you need, you can call me and ask for help."

Mark was so happy that he forgot about the pandemic and hugged him, saying, "Thank you very much! God bless you."

The man smiled and said, "I'm already very blessed by God.

Because of it, I help other people."

Joanna said, "Only out of curiosity, do you have any religion?"

'Yes, I have. I'm Catholic. And during my whole life, I learned that helping my neighbor is the greatest commandment given by Jesus. And I try to follow it every day."

"It's a pity that not everyone thinks like that."

"It's really a pity. The world would be a much better place."

"For sure. One more time, thank you very much for everything."

"I'm available for what you need. I'm gonna buy the things and ask the supermarket to deliver them to you."

Mark replied, "Thank you."

The man went to the supermarket, and they followed their way. They were happy because they got the necessary help.

It is not the Devil's Fault

1

On a sunny afternoon, two men walked down a quiet street, John and his pastor Matthew.

John was a white man with tan skin, average height, thin shape, short dark brown hair, and light brown eyes. He says in a sad tone, "Pastor Matthew, my life is too bad!"

The pastor was a middle-aged light brown man, average height, thin, with brown hair almost shaved and light brown eyes. He got scared and asked, "What happened? What's the problem?"

"Pastor, unfortunately, it's not a problem, but many problems."

"Tell me, John, what's bothering you?"

"Pastor, I've suffered a lot lately." John says in an anguished tone, "Everything is going wrong in my life."

"Mercy on you! Everything?" The pastor was surprised.

'Yes, everything. My marriage is very bad. My wife and I fight all the time; we can't even talk."

"John, marriage is made by two persons; you two must sit down and talk about what is happening and what you need to improve."

"But pastor, we've already tried this, and didn't work."

"Then, maybe you must seek help from an expert. We have a couples' ministry in our church. They always can help."

"I'm sure that this won't work!" John stated categorically.

"How are you so sure?"

"Pastor, this is the enemy's work. He is attempting against my life."

Matthew was very surprised about John's speech because he knew he had no dialogue with his wife.

"Are you sure that is Satan's work?"

"Of course, pastor! He wants to destroy me."

"In fact, John, the Devil tries to destroy all true Christians."

"It's because of this that he is against me." John says with conviction, "I'm a true Christian!"

Again, Matthew looks with distrust because he knew that John was not so good like that.

"Of course, you're a good Christian. You're excellent, a piece of pure gold jewelry from Ophir[9] in our church," Replies Matthew ironically.

John continued with his statements, "Besides my marriage, the Devil has risen in other areas of my life."

Matthew replied doubtfully, "Really? Which areas?"

"Look, pastor Matthew, in my work the Devil wants me to be fired, and then, I'll stop giving tithe and the offerings in the church. Everything is a strategy."

"Are you sure that is really the Devil?"

"Of course!" John replied confidently.

"I'm questioning because, maybe, it can be something related to

---

[9] Name of a region mentioned in the Bible, famous for its wealth. 1st Kings 9:28, 10:11, 22:48.

your productivity and performance in the company and not a Devil's work."

"No way, pastor! I'm an exemplary employee."

Matthew knew that John was not so good like that, so, he agreed with him to avoid conflicts, "Yes, you're very dedicated to all your works."

"Another thing, pastor, besides taking out my job, he wants to destroy my finances. He is sending the devourer[10] to run out my wage. There are many debts and little money to pay."

"John, don't you think the debts can be related to the fact that you're always purchasing many things you don't need? For example, you change your cell phone every two months, and every year, you purchase a more expensive car than the previous one."

John smiled and said, "But pastor Matthew, my spending is according to my wage. And as a Christian, I have the right to enjoy the best from the land[11]."

"John, the word of God isn't exactly in these terms. Be careful with your interpretation. It's necessary to study the scriptures to know

---

[10] Some Christians believe that there exists a Devil named "devourer", who is responsible for the destruction of people and their wealth.
This belief arose from a mistaken interpretation of a text in the book of Malachi, 3:11. The complete text talks about a reprehension against Israel's people because of their sins. The mentioned devourer is a kind of locust that would destroy the vegetation.
[11] Another mistaken interpretation of a biblical text, Isaiah 1:19. The context is about one piece of advice from God to Israel's people, where God says what will happen to them if they obey (blessings) and if they do not obey (destruction).

the true will of God for our lives. If you participated more in the services and biblical classes, you'd have more knowledge."

"But pastor, it's the Devil who prevents me from going more to the church."

"The Devil? Are you sure?"

"Of course! He always creates obstacles for me not to go."

"John, I know you, and I know that in the days of the service, you're always on some ride, and because of it you don't go."

John tried to justify himself, "Pastor Matthew, I try to go, but I can't."

"All right, it's like you say. Is there anything else that the Devil bothers you about?"

"Yes, there is. I have many health problems. Respiratory infections, high cholesterol, and glucose levels; there are too many problems."

"John, some diseases are caused by our daily life; for example, cholesterol and glucose are related to food."

John replied with discouragement, "I know it pastor, and I know the enemy is attempting strongly against me."

Matthew was a little impatient with John's excuses and asked, "Is there anything else that you remember?"

"Look, pastor, at the moment, there isn't. I wanna you to pray for me, to rebuke these demons that attempt against my life."

"Alright. Let's pray."

They give the hands, and Matthew starts to pray, "Sovereign Lord, bless the life of your servant John. May the Lord be with him all days, ridding, protecting, and guarding him against all evils. May the Lord grant to your servant wisdom, intelligence, and understanding all days of his life. Help him in all his difficulties every day, in Jesus' name. Amen."

John went away dissatisfied with the pastor's words, who did not believe that everything in his life was the Devil's work.

2

One night, John knelt in his bedroom to pray, "Oh, Lord, my life is so hard; it seems that everything and everyone is against me," John prayed, sadly and dismayed.

"My marriage is going from bad to worse. My job is hanging by a thread. My financial life is a mess, and it seems like everything is getting worse."

John raises his voice and says, "But I'm sure that everything is the fault of the enemy, Satan. He has stolen my blessings and taken away my peace and tranquility."

John continues firmly, "The Devil doesn't rest, and he is always attempting against the true sons of God. Lord, rebuke this evil in my life! Deliver me from everything bad that he attempts against me! I cry out for the removal of all Devil's curses in Jesus' name."

While he was praying, John heard the bell of his house and went to answer. Before opening the gate, he asked, "Who is?"

A male voice says, "Is this John's house?"

"Yes, who wants to talk with him?"

"I'm a person who is very sad with you. Because you have criticized me too much."

John was surprised about this speech because he did not criticize anyone to the point of making the person sad, "Did I criticize you? Are you sure?"

"Of course!"

"Who are you?"

"Let me enter, then, I'm gonna explain to you."

"Alright."

John opened the gate and was admired by the person. It was a very handsome man; very well-dressed in elegant clothes, with a great presentation. He seemed like a fashion model or an actor.

John did not recognize him and said in surprise, "Who are you? I don't know you."

"You know me. You talk about me every day," the person said in a mysterious tone.

"I don't know you."

"Everyone always says it. I'm the Devil."

John laughed out loud and said, "The Devil? You?" John continued laughing.

"Don't you believe it?"

"What kind of Devil are you? The sales' Devil? Or the Devil of a dark metal group?"

'I'm none of them. I'm the Devil, demon, Satan, Beelzebub, the prince of darkness."

John continued without believing in it. Then, the Devil said, "Human beings are all the same, they don't believe when they hear the truth."

One big darkness surrounded them, and all the lights turned off. He said with a potent and evil voice, "I'm the great dragon! The Revelation Beast. The destructor, the enemy, I'm the personification of all evil."

The lights turned on, and John got extremely terrified. He was trembling and with a horror expression. He said with a trembling voice, "Oh, my God! You really are the Devil! I order that you get out here, Devil from hell."

Nothing happened, and the Devil said, ironically, "Wrong words. Try again."

John cried out desperately, "Jesus Christ has mercy on me!"

Then, Jesus appeared on John's side and said, "John, did you call me?"

John replied euphorically, "Yes, Lord! Have mercy on me! The Devil appeared for me!"

Jesus said reproachfully, "Why didn't you rebuke him with the power that was given to you?"

"I rebuked him, but he didn't obey."

"But you have rebuked him in the wrong way, you said, 'I order that you get out here, Devil from hell.' You didn't say that you would rebuke him in my name. You wanted to rebuke him in your own authority."

"But Lord! In your word, it is written that it was given authority to your disciples."

"It really is written like this. But the authority is in my name, Jesus Christ, and not in your own words. If you had sought more knowledge in the bible, you would know it."

John was without a reply; he bowed down and said with humility, "Forgive me, Lord, I'm poor and needy of your mercy and love."

Jesus replied with satisfaction, "Now you behaved like a true God's servant."

John got up and said, "Lord, I have a doubt." ,

"Tell me."

"I thought that the Devil was ugly, do you know? That thing of horns, tail, and trident. So, I thought he would appear in the likeness of a horror movie. But he appeared like that, well-dressed." John pointed to the Devil.

Jesus replied, "John, this doubt, he will explain."

The Devil began to talk with an air of superiority, "John, I, the Devil, always show my better face when I want to conquer people. These stories that I'm ugly are a big lie. If I was ugly, nobody would come to me and would do my will." The Devil gets close to John and says, "I have many faces, including one of a very beautiful woman, if you are interested…"

John got interested and said, "A very beautiful woman, oh, really?"

Jesus looked at John and said reproachfully, "People get carried away to the evil path because of so little."

John tried to justify, "Don't, Lord Jesus! I was only curious; I wouldn't get carried away."

Jesus replied firmly, "John, don't try to deceive me nor deceive yourself, I know the deepest intentions of your heart."

John kept silent and thoughtful.

The Devil bowed down before Jesus and said, "Excuse me, Lord."

Jesus turns to him and says, "Satan, why do you disturb me?"

Satan says reproachfully, "Lord, your servant is defaming me. He's making accusations of things that I didn't think nor did against him!"

John interrupted, exalted, "Don't believe in him, Lord! He is the father of lies!"

Jesus replied firmly, "Stay quiet, John! I know everything! You, in the condition of a sinner, do you want to teach how to be a Christian?"

John got ashamed and replied, "Forgive me, Lord. It was only a force of habit."

Jesus continued, "Satan, what did you say is related to the problems of his life that he always says are your fault?"

"Exactly this, Lord Jesus!"

John got exalted and interrupted again, "It's his fault! Everything bad that happens in my life is the enemy's work."

The Devil retorts, "Do I look like a builder to do work in the life of others? Huh, everyone has their own problems."

John continued firmly, "Liar!"

Jesus interrupts him and says, "John, stay quiet now!"

"Alright, Lord," John replied with fear.

Jesus continued, "John, I know all your thoughts and understand that you really believe the Devil is guilty of your situation. As much as he is always disposed to kill, steal, and destroy. However, many things are consequences of your actions and decisions."

The Devil said, "Now that Jesus has spoken, I hope you believe."

Jesus said, "As much as I'm speaking, I know he still didn't believe faithfully. Therefore, I'm going to show him."

The Devil said nervously, "This human race is very incredulous! From the beginning, everything must be revealed in the smallest details. Only the Lord and his Father have patience with them."

John did not understand Jesus' words and asked, "Lord, to show me? How?"

"John, tell me how your life is. And we'll see what justifies each situation."

"Alright, Lord. My life is very hard. My marriage is too complicated; my job is hanging by a thread. I have too many debts; the devourer is ruining me. I always have many obstacles for going to church and participating in the work. And my health is too poor. And whose fault is all this? Of the Devil!"

The Devil replied angrily, "Jesus, these your children always do the same thing! They need to blame others. It started in the Garden of Eden, Adam blamed Eve, and she blamed the serpent. It's incredible how they always get some excuse to justify their own mistakes…"

"Satan, I know all of it!" Jesus said. "My Father and I still love them, and this is something you'll never understand."

John replied, "Then, Lord, what I said is not all the fault of the Devil?"

"John, let's analyze each thing you said. Firstly, you said about your marriage. Let's call someone too important to testify about your words. Vivian, come here, please."

She suddenly appeared. A very beautiful woman, with light brown skin, average height, a body in good shape, curly hair shoulder-length, and blue eyes. She bows down before Jesus and says, "Here is your servant, Lord."

She got up, turned to Satan, and said with authority, "I rcbukc you demon! Go back to hell in the name of Jesus!"

And Satan disappeared crying out, "Noooooo!"

John said, "My love, how did you know he was Satan?"

"The Holy Spirit revealed me."

Jesus said to Vivian, "Very well, faithful servant. But he was here with my permission. Satan, you can come back."

Satan went back raging, "These servants of Jesus always do the same thing! They always send me to hell. It's too hard!"

Jesus continued, "How is your marriage?"

Vivian said, discouraged, "My Lord Jesus!" Vivian sighed. "Things are very complicated. John virtually doesn't talk with me. When he arrives from the job, he neither kisses me nor says he loves me and doesn't do anything to please me."

"And does he always behave like that?"

"Yes, Lord. It's always the same thing. He arrives complaining about everything. He neither notices me nor what I make for him. Every day, he sits on the sofa and stays the entire time on the phone talking to some women from his work. There are moments that it seems they are more important than me."

"Besides that, what more does he do or doesn't do?"

"Lord, he never praises me, never says any kindle word to me. He only wants to complain and curse me. He is always saying I don't know how to do anything, and that I should learn with his mother. And the worst, when we walk in the street, he keeps noticing all the women. He does it blatantly. He is so shameless that if he saw a goat in a skirt, he could find it beautiful and keep looking at it."

John was impressed by the words of his wife.

Jesus hugged Vivian and said confidently, "My daughter, thank you very much for your words. Go in peace, and don't give up.

Your husband will change."

"Thank you very much, my Lord."

Vivian disappeared.

Jesus continued, "John, where did the Devil participate in all this? I didn't see any action from him. Everything that happened, you did it by your own will."

John was without a reply and tried to justify, "But Lord! It's… The body… Is… Weak."

"John, I said, 'Watch and pray so that you will not fall into temptation. The spirit is willing, but the body is weak[12]. I said to watch and pray to fortify yourself. I don't say this for you to have an excuse to get carried away by the desires."

Satan says to John, "I said that I'm not responsible for what happens in your life."

John replies embarrassed, "At this point, you're right."

And Jesus says, "Let's analyze the next situation you said, your job."

"Lord!" John said with affliction, "There are many fights and persecution there."

Satan said, ironically, "This has another name."

Jesus said, "Let's talk with your superior to see what he says. Alexander, please, come here."

---

[12] Matthew 26:41, Mark 14:38.
In these two texts, Jesus highlights the importance of being alert and praying in every situation. The spirit is willing to do everything, but the physical body is weak and can fall into temptation.

He suddenly appeared. A middle-aged white man with very fair skin, tall, a little overweight, light brown short hair, and light brown eyes. He bows down before Jesus and says, "Here is your servant, Lord."

He got up, turned to Satan, and said with authority, "I rebuke you, Satan! Go back to the depths of hell in the name of Jesus!"

Satan disappeared crying out, "Noooooo!"

John said, "Alexander, how did you know he was Satan?"

"The Holy Spirit revealed me."

Jesus said to Alexander, "Very well, faithful servant. But he was here with my permission. Satan, you can come back."

Satan returned complaining, "They expelled me again! It's hard to have a reasonable conversation today."

Jesus said to Alexander, "How is John's work?"

"Look, Lord. John is a good employee. However, he doesn't accomplish his duty."

"Can you explain to us better?"

"Of course! Look, almost all days he arrives delayed; he does not commit to the time. And he always uses the same excuse: 'There was terrible traffic!'" he said ironically. "Or he says: "My car broke.' Lord, I try to understand his side, but he's the employee who lives closer to the company and is the one who has more delays."

"Besides that, Alexander, how about his performance?"

"When he wants, he works very well. He makes everything at the right time without mistakes and still adds something besides what was required. But when he doesn't want to… Huh… There is no way; he delays, says that it's very hard, and delivers the job incomplete."

"And do you think about firing him?"

"Lord, unfortunately, it's a possibility. Even other employees feel uncomfortable about his behavior. Everyone asks why he is still employed. I'm trying to control people's reactions and give him one more chance to see if he improves."

Jesus hugged Alexander and said confidently, "Thank you very much for your information. Go in peace, and don't give up. John will improve."

"Thank you very much, Lord."

Alexander disappeared.

Satan said ironically, "Again, it's not my fault your bad life. It's yourself who seeks your own problems."

John got very constrained and did not have a reply.

Jesus said, "John, it's like that in the Scriptures: 'If a man will not work, he shall not eat[13].' You need commitment to your work and don't be lazy and careless. This is a terrible testimony for a Christian."

---

[13] 2nd Thessalonians 3:10. The apostle Paul highlights the importance of the work as a manner to keep self-sustenance. Those who do not want to work, cannot eat.

"But Lord!"

"But nothing! You're wrong and know it. Don't try to make lame excuses."

John downed his head and said, discouraged, "Alright, Lord. I recognize my fault."

"Very well. This is the beginning of your change. Let's continue with what you said, 'I have too many debts, the devourer is ruining me.'"

"Ha! Ha! Ha!" Satan interrupted, laughing out loud, and said, "Lord Jesus, does he really believe wholeheartedly in this story of devourer and that I'm responsible for his doubts?"

"Yes, Satan. He believes firmly in this."

"Ha! Ha! Ha!' Satan laughed loud again and said, "I'm obligated to hear such absurdity. If I didn't know him, I would think he doesn't have a Bible and an excellent pastor to explain it to him."

John was displeased about Satan's words and said, "But Lord, the blame is on him! Even giving my tithe and offerings. He is attacking me, preventing me from enjoying the best of this land."

'Ha! Ha! Ha!' Satan laughed out loud again and said, "Sorry Lord, I couldn't contain myself."

"John," Jesus said, "Things don't work like that. Giving tithes and offerings doesn't prevent the money from being spent irresponsibly. And to enjoy the best of this land requires too much hard work, a thing that we've already seen that you don't do."

John got ashamed and said discouraged, "Yes, Lord. I understand."

"Let's analyze your financial life to clarify what is happening. To help us, I'll call Roderick, your best friend. Roderick, please, come here."

He suddenly appeared. A black man, about the same age as John, with dark brown skin, tall, thin, short black hair, and dark brown eyes. He bows down before Jesus and says, "Here is your servant, Lord."

He got up, turned to Satan, and said with authority,

"I rebuke you, demon! Go back to hell in the name of Jesus!"

And Satan disappeared, crying out, "Again, noooooo!"

John said angrily, "Lord, there is no way the Holy Spirit has revealed to him about Satan, my friend is Catholic!"

Jesus shook his head negatively and said, "Besides everything wrong you do, you still have this kind of thought. He has true faith in me and my Father. And it was the Holy Spirit who revealed everything to him."

Jesus said to Roderick, "Very well, faithful servant. But he was here with my permission. Satan, you can come back."

Satan returned complaining again, "Every time, someone sends me to hell. In this way, it's very complicated."

Jesus said to Roderick, "How do you describe John's financial life?"

Roderick sighed and said, "Lord, he's too complicated."

"Complicated? Explain it better."

"John is a good person, a close friend, but there are moments he seems addicted to buying. Virtually every month, he appears with a new cell phone, and this isn't because the older one has broken or something like that; all is because he wants to be in fashion and up to date with the latest release."

"Besides cell phones, does he buy anything else unnecessary?"

"Yes, Lord. He buys too many unnecessary things. John buys much more shoes than he needs. I think he is reaching about thirty pairs. Clothing, only of expensive brands, he even bought a pair of pants that cost almost a month's salary. And the most serious and expensive, he changes his car every year."

"How do you think this harms John?"

"He can't pay any bills on time; he always pays when there are two or three overdue bills. Because of this, his wife is always arguing with him. But he never listens to her and never changes. It's a very complicated situation."

"I got it."

Jesus hugged Roderick and said confidently, "Thank you very much for your clarification. Go in peace, and don't give up. John will improve."

"Thank you, Lord."

Roderick disappeared.

Satan said to John accusing him, "You are accusing me of being the devourer of your money, but the true devourer here is you! Wasting your money in this way no salary can stand it."

John looked at Jesus hoping He would say something comforting, and Jesus said reproachfully, "John, there's no use doing this poor guy expression. You haven't the minimum responsibility for your money's administration. You seem like a child in a toy store; everything you see, you want to take."

John replied, discouraged, "It's true, Lord, I have no discipline about my money. I need to improve."

Noticing that everything in his life was the fault of his own actions, John requested to Jesus, "Lord, I already saw that everything that is happening is my own responsibility, I think we can stop here."

"No way!" Satan interrupted furiously. "You accused and slandered me. Now is the time for you to be confronted with the truth."

"But Lord!" John said, looking at Jesus. "I already learned my lesson."

Jesus replied, "John, at this moment, you've learned part of the lesson; it's necessary to continue until the end of what you said for you to learn everything."

John replied discouraged, "Yes, Lord."

Jesus continued, "Let's see what you do for your health to be too poor. For this analysis, it's you who will clarify for us."

"Alright, Lord."

"John, when was the last time you went to a doctor?"

John did not understand the reason for the question, "The Lord already knows everything. Why do I have to reply?"

"You need to reply to yourself and listen to what you are doing. Then, you'll understand the reason to be like that."

"Alright, Lord. I went to see a doctor about five years ago."

Jesus made a surprised expression and said, "Five years? It's too much time. In this way, you can't monitor your health. You should go to the doctor at least once a year or when you feel something is wrong."

"It's true, Lord."

"And how do you describe your eating?"

"Lord, I eat almost everything, except fruits and vegetables; I don't like them. I prefer meat, sandwiches, and candies, and when I purchase vegetables, I like potato and cassava fried. Food to sustain me."

"But you know this kind of eating is damaging to your health. You need to eat healthy foods for your body to be well nourished with vitamins."

John got thoughtful and said, "It's true, Lord."

"John, do you exercise?"

"I don't, Lord."

"Let's see how your life is. You don't go to the doctor, don't eat healthy food, don't exercise. It's because of it that your health is in this way."

Satan interrupted, "John, give thanks to Jesus for still being alive. Some people already are hospitalized and even die for much less. It's because of God's mercy that you are still alive."

Jesus says, "You're seeing. Even he knows how to recognize God's love in people's lives. You should do the same."

John noticed one more time his life was like that because of his own attitude.

Jesus said, "Now, let's analyze the last piece of your speech, the lack of time to seek God."

Satan said, "This one is farther from God than he thinks."

Recognizing his own mistakes, John says humbly, "Lord, I know that I'm not a good Christian and need to improve in many aspects. I ask you for a bit more mercy and patience because I'll change. Now, show me what I'm doing wrong."

Jesus was admired by John's words and said, "John, now you truly learned about your responsibility. To finish, let's call your pastor to clarify your lack of time to seek God. Matthew, please, come here."

He suddenly appeared, bowed down before Jesus, and said, "Lord Jesus, here is your servant."

He got up and looked at Satan; this one thought, Here we go again. When he would rebuke him, Jesus interrupted, "Matthew, there is no need to rebuke him. He's here with my permission. And only today, he has already been sent to hell three times."

"Alright, Lord."

Satan said relieved, "Phew. If one more sent me to hell, I wouldn't return."

John was amazed about it and said, "Pastor Matthew, how did you know he was Satan?"

"As soon as I arrived, the Holy Spirit revealed to me that he was the Devil."

"When I saw him, I didn't recognize him as the Devil, and when I tried to rebuke him, he didn't leave my presence."

Matthew replies ironically, "I can't even imagine the reason."

Jesus said, "Matthew, we're here in a kind of audience about John's life."

"Is the audience because of John's claims about the enemy's attacks on his life?"

"Exactly this!"

John was amazed and asked, "How did you know it, pastor? Did the Holy Spirit reveal it to you too?"

"No, this I deduced from what I know about you. You are always complaining about the enemy in your life, and you never stop and think about your own attitude. I'm always saying it, but you don't believe it."

"It's true, pastor, you're right. Jesus showed me how much I'm guilty of what happens in my life. I learned my lesson."

"This is great. I would like you to have listened to me when I said."

Jesus said, "Matthew, now, tell me about John's Christian life."

"Yes, Lord. John is Christian like Silvio Santos[14] because he only appears on Sundays, and sometimes, not even that. He always has appointments at the time of the activities in the church. One time, he didn't go to Wednesday's service because the match of his favorite soccer team was at the same time."

"I got it. Besides this, does he fail in anything else?"

'Yes, he does. He never goes to biblical school. Another thing he often does is take isolated texts in the Bible and try to apply them to his life in a literal sense. It's clear he did not even seek to read the Bible to understand the context."

Jesus hugged Matthew and said with confidence, "Thank you very much. Don't give up. He will improve."

"Thank you, Lord."

Matthew looked at Satan, and so looked at Jesus. This one said, "Yes, you can do it, Matthew."

Satan says, "Here we go again!"

Matthew rebuked Satan, "In the name of Jesus! Go back to hell!"

Satan disappeared crying out, "Noooooo!"

Matthew disappeared.

"John, we analyzed all the aspects of your life. And you saw for

---

[14] Silvio Santos is the most famous talk show presenter in Brazil. He always has hosted shows on Sundays.

yourself that everything that happens is a consequence of your acts. Then, change your attitude to have a different life, because one day, maybe it will be too late…"

Jesus began to walk, and John tried to follow him, but he could not.

John pleaded to Jesus, "Lord, come back, I need your help!"

"John, I will always be with you; you only need to know how to listen to my voice…

Acknowledgements

The following sites contain a lot of useful information for translating.

Behind the Name

Google Docs

Google Translator

Grammarly

Oxford Dictionary

Wikipedia

I thank the site Pexels and the author Pixabay for the base picture of the cover.

Special acknowledgement

I thank God. He gave me the intelligence to write the book.

About the author

Rafael Henrique dos Santos Lima

Associate Degree in Administration and M.B.A. in Strategic Project Management by Centro Universitário UNA. Christian by the grace of God. Passionate about writing (English, Portuguese, Spanish), poet and novelist.

Contacts

rafael50001@hotmail.com

rafaelhsts@gmail.com

Blog: escritorrafaellima.blogspot.com